Chime Travelers #1

Advance praise for *The Secret of the Shamrock*

"Lisa Hendey has always had the ability to inspire and lead other Catholic moms. Now, with the warmth and care of an experienced mother, she demonstrates her ability to offer inspiration to their children, too."

—Jared Dees, author, *31 Days to Becoming a Better Religious Educator*

"Here is a whimsical series that will capture young readers' imaginations while feeding their souls. Hendey has created a fantastical adventure series with a conscience that reminds readers of all ages that with God all things are possible."

—Kate Wicker, author, *Weightless: Making Peace With Your Body*

"Lisa Hendey's Chime Travelers series delivers Catholic values in an entertaining fashion that will delight the young and young at heart. This father of five can't wait for the next volume."

—Pete Socks, the Catholic Book Blogger

"Lisa Hendey loves her faith, and that love shines through in this book. Young readers will be entertained without realizing they're also learning a little more what it means to be a Catholic."

—Rachel Balducci, author, *How Do You Tuck In a Superhero*

"I read aloud the first book of Lisa Hendey's delightful new series to my third grade students. They loved the story. They said the book was 'Saint-tastic,' and they gave it five snaps and jazz hands!"

—Barb Gilman, third grade teacher, St. Mary Margaret School, Omaha, Nebraska

servant

AN IMPRINT OF
FRANCISCAN MEDIA
Cincinnati, Ohio

The Secret of
the Shamrock

LISA M. HENDEY
ILLUSTRATED BY JENN BOWER

Much of the dialogue in this book between Patrick and St. Patrick is inspired by quotations from St. Patrick's Confessio. For more about St. Patrick, see page 113.

Cover and book design by Mark Sullivan
All illustrations by Jenn Bower

Library of Congress Control Number: 2015936958
ISBN 978-1-61636-847-0

Published by Servant,
an imprint of Franciscan Media
28 W. Liberty St.
Cincinnati, OH 45202
www.FranciscanMedia.org

Printed in the United States of America.
Printed on acid-free paper.
16 17 18 19 5 4 3

▲ Chapter One ▲

The adventure started one cold Saturday afternoon at St. Anne's parish.

Clang, clang, clang… chimed the big bells in the church tower.

Every day—in the morning, at noon and at night—those loud old bells rang nine times. For almost one hundred years, they had been chiming that way every day.

The big, bronze bells of St. Anne's were so loud that they could be heard from miles away. And sometimes, when those bells rang, amazing things happened.

That snowy Saturday morning, as the first bell chimed, a little tree frog named Francis woke up from the nap he was taking. As the second bell chimed, Francis decided he wanted to go for a swim. And as the third bell chimed Francis's green eyes spied a big bowl of cool water that looked very refreshing…

Splash!

"What were you thinking, Patrick?" Mom whispered as the bells finished their ninth chime. Dad tried to fish the small tree frog out of the water but the frog was slippery. Francis slipped out of his hands and back into the big bowl of holy water. Patrick could have sworn that he saw Francis smile as his little frog legs carried him across the baptismal font.

Patrick's twin sister, Katie, couldn't hold back a giggle. Once Katie started laughing, little baby Hoa Hong, adorable in her white baptismal gown, smiled too. Before long, everyone in the church was laughing.

Everyone except Patrick, who knew he was about to get in trouble. Again.

In the end, St. Anne's pastor Father Miguel managed to catch Francis the frog just as he was hopping out of the cold water.

"I think this little guy must belong to you," the priest said, handing the frog to Patrick.

"Great catch!" Patrick whispered. "Thanks, Father." He tucked the small creature back into the front pocket of his dress pants.

Watching Father Miguel pour water over little Hoa Hong's head and recite the baptismal prayers, Patrick thought about his family. For so long, the Brady twins had wished and prayed for a younger brother or sister. And finally, God had answered their prayers. Only a few months ago, their family had adopted Hoa Hong, their little sister. "Rosebud," as they sometimes called her, had come all the way from Vietnam to become a part of the Brady family.

Patrick and Katie had a special bond. They read the same books and played the same games. Both hated broccoli and loved sushi. They traded chores, rode bikes together, and helped each other with homework. Katie loved Religion and Spelling. Patrick was a math whiz. They were in the same class at St. Anne's School and helped each other with homework.

They both had red hair, bright green eyes, and lots of freckles. Katie was a little taller than Patrick. Patrick was less shy than Katie. And while they fought sometimes, the twins were best friends. All in all, the Brady twins made a great team.

But there were a few things about Patrick that Katie had a hard time understanding.

And bringing a tree frog to a baptism was one of them!

▲ Chapter Two ▲

A week later, Patrick and Katie were sitting together in the backseat of the red van, on their way back to St. Anne's again.

"Why did you even have Francis in your pocket anyway?" Katie asked. She and Patrick loved animals. Katie even liked Francis. She just didn't like him going to church, especially when it meant that both twins had to go back the next Saturday for Patrick's punishment!

"We've already been over this, Katie," Mom said with a sigh.

"Yeah, it's history!" shouted Patrick over Hoa Hong's cries.

"It may be history, but it was still stupid," Katie yelled back. "Who brings a tree frog to a baptism?"

"I told you," growled Patrick, "Francis is just a little guy. I didn't want to leave him at home."

Next to him, Katie nodded. She knew that Patrick was doing a great job of feeding and caring for Francis. But she still wasn't happy about giving up her Saturday.

"But you have to admit," Patrick laughed, "Francis is a pretty good jumper! I can't believe he made it all the way from my pocket into that bowl of water!"

"It's not a bowl!" Katie rolled her eyes. "It's a *font*. And that frog pretty much ruined Hoa Hong's special day."

"Now, Katie," Mom said from the front seat, trying to hold back her own laugh, "The day wasn't ruined. It's a good thing that Father Miguel was so fast to catch Francis."

Mom still thought it was funny that Patrick named his pet after Pope Francis.

"Besides, I don't think any of us will ever forget Hoa Hong's baptism. But Dad and I have been talking. We both agree that we could all benefit from some time spent learning more about our church. We go to Mass every Sunday, but there is still so much for us to discover there."

"But, Mom," grumbled Patrick. "Back at church on another Saturday? Two weeks in a row? And we have to go again tomorrow for Mass?"

As he said this, Patrick put his hand over a bulge in the front pocket of his favorite hooded sweatshirt. Inside that pocket, Francis was quiet—*for now*. Patrick hoped he'd stay that way, at least until they got out of the van. *He's still a baby,* Patrick thought. *I'll just keep him away from the font this time.*

"You're lucky that all Mom is making you do is volunteer to clean the church, Patrick!" said Katie from her seat next to Hoa Hong. "If I were in charge, I'd take away your Master Blaster game for a month!"

"Well, you're not in charge!" teased Patrick. "And watch out, or Francis may end up in the tub with you when you least expect it!"

"Gross!"

"Waaahhhh!" cried Hoa Hong.

"Kids! Please…" begged Mom. "We're here!"

The van pulled into the big, empty parking lot at St. Anne's. Patrick thought it was a little spooky to walk into the dark old church. Mom said they only had to stay and clean for an hour. Then he and Francis could head out to find his buddies at the creek.

▲ Chapter Three ▲

"This is so cool," whispered Katie as she genuflected, dropping to one knee in front of the tabernacle. "We have the church all to ourselves!"

"You're such a holy roller, Katie," Patrick said, rolling his eyes. Katie was such a kiss-up about church. She was always giving Patrick advice like, "Pray about it," or "Offer your worry to God." It was so annoying. *Easy for her to say,* Patrick thought. *She's almost as preachy as Father Miguel these days!* "Let's just do this and get out of here fast. We already have to come back tomorrow."

"Ribbit," agreed Francis, from the front pocket of Patrick's hoodie. He, too, would have rather been at the creek!

Mrs. Danks, the lady who was in charge of the Saturday "Cleaning Team" at St. Anne's, greeted them from behind the altar.

"Welcome," she said in a cheery voice. Patrick loved Mrs. Danks because she smelled like fresh-baked bread and loved to sing the latest country music hits.

"Why does Mrs. Danks sound so funny, Mom?" Patrick whispered. The only thing he knew about the old lady was that she made awesome brownies. He was pretty sure Mrs. Danks was as old as the bells of St. Anne's.

"She's Irish, Patrick," Mom whispered back.

"Well we're Irish, too, but Mrs. Danks sounds different…"

"She was born there, Patrick," Mom said quietly. "Which is why she still has her beautiful accent."

"Oh, Patrick," Mrs. Danks called out with her Irish accent. "Won't you come here, please? I have a treat for you."

Awesome, Patrick thought to himself, remembering to bow this time as he crossed behind the altar. *I think I smell chocolate!*

The bells of St. Anne's chimed nine times, ringing the noon Angelus prayer. Patrick paused, transfixed by the ringing that was so loud that it almost made the church rumble. And for a moment Patrick forgot that he'd been mad about going to church.

"Ribbit," sang Francis, who also liked the smell of chocolate and the sound of bells. He definitely seemed to agree!

▲ Chapter Four ▲

Bbrriiinnngggg!

"Finally, 10:15!" said Patrick, greeting the recess bell with relief as he grabbed a soccer ball on his way out the classroom door. "I thought that Religion lesson would never be over…"

"What's wrong, Patrick?" teased his buddy Pedro. "Does all that talk about the sacrament of confession make you *nervous*?"

"He should be nervous," said Katie from a nearby spot on the soccer field. "Patrick has a pretty long list of sins right now."

Nearby, Katie's best friends, Maria and Erin, giggled.

"Let's get out of here, Pedro!" yelled Patrick, kicking the soccer ball to the far end of the field.

When they finally caught up with the ball, Pedro turned to Patrick. "Dude, why were you so late getting to the creek on Saturday? We almost gave up on you."

Patrick wasn't quite ready to tell Pedro that Mom had volunteered him to spend *every* Saturday for the rest of the school year cleaning the church. Saturdays were supposed to be for soccer, basketball, or baseball games or hanging out at the creek. They were not supposed to be spent in some creepy old building that smelled like incense.

"About that confession thing, Patrick," Pedro stopped, grabbing the ball. "I know Katie was teasing you, but you're not really nervous, right?

I mean, we've done it before…so what's the big deal? You go in, sit down with Father Miguel for a few minutes, say your stuff, and get out. And then you're good to go until next year."

"But, Pedro," interrupted Gregory, who was standing at the edge of the field. "That's not exactly the right spirit for the sacrament of reconciliation. It's a gift, something that we should approach prayerfully and with respect."

"Well, thanks for the religion lesson, future

Father Gregory!" Patrick sneered. "Who asked you?"

In his heart, Patrick knew he was being mean to Gregory, but he couldn't help himself. Even though Gregory was an altar server and the smartest brainiac in class, he was still pretty cool. But Patrick wasn't in the mood for another religion lesson.

"And besides, how would you know?" Patrick snarled. "The only sin you've ever been cool enough to do is being a huge know-it-all. Why don't you just go read your *Catechism!*"

He felt badly the minute the words came out of his mouth, but he ignored his guilt for the rest of recess. He tried not to look at Gregory, who stood next to the field looking like he was about to cry.

▲ Chapter Five ▲

"Aren't you even a little bit nervous when you go?" Patrick whispered to Katie from the backseat of the van.

It was Saturday again, and they were on their way back to St. Anne's for the weekly cleaning. Patrick hoped the hour would pass quickly and that it would end with one of Mrs. Danks's double-chocolate brownies.

"It's a *gift*, Patrick," Katie whispered back, not wanting to embarrass her twin in front of Dad. Dr. Brady was off duty from the hospital today and taking his turn on the Cleaning Team.

"Remember how we learned that it's a sign of God's grace and love for us?" Katie asked. "When we confess our sins to the priest and do the penance he gives us, God always forgives us. No matter how bad, or dumb, or mean we might be…"

Patrick thought about that for a minute, remembering how mean he had been to Gregory the other day. His stomach fluttered. Did he really have to tell Father Miguel about that?

"But yeah," Katie admitted quietly, "I get nervous too. Honestly, I'm pretty sure everyone does!"

Knowing that Katie got nervous helped a little bit. In his head, Patrick knew that Katie was right. But in his heart, he was still pretty freaked out about going in and telling Father Miguel all of the bad stuff he had done. He didn't want to think about confession right now. He just wanted to get in, dust the pews, and get out to the creek as soon as possible.

"Ribbit!" said Francis from the front pocket of Patrick's blue backpack.

"We're here, guys!" announced Dad. "Since this is my first time, you're going to have to show me the ropes."

"Don't worry, Daddy," Katie said with a giggle. "Mrs. Danks will take care of that!"

Patrick laughed too. This wasn't exactly his first choice for the father-son time Dad usually planned for the two of them. Now that Hoa Hong was around and the girls outnumbered the boys at the Brady house, the two of them had to stick together!

But Patrick still thought the idea of Dad taking his turn on the Cleaning Team was pretty cool. Dad was a convert. Both twins remembered watching last Easter Vigil as their father had been baptized, confirmed, and received his First Holy Communion. It had been a special moment for all of the Bradys. And now Dad kept learning about his Catholic faith right along with his twins.

"Well, look who's here to help us clean!" Dad grinned, fist-bumping Father Miguel. "I'm surprised you're not too tired to clean after that beating I gave you on the basketball court this morning."

"Hey, old man," Father Miguel teased. "I was taking it easy on you. And Mrs. Danks isn't feeling well today. So now we'll see who is really in charge! You'd better not miss any spots while I'm leading the Cleaning Team. Maybe I should put your dad on bathroom duty, kids—what do you think?"

"You're going to clean the church with us, Father Miguel?" Katie asked.

"Sure!" he said, smiling. "This is my home, too! And you should see me with a vacuum cleaner!" The twins watched as Father Miguel began dancing around with an imaginary vacuum. "Wait till you catch my new moves!"

"Don't tell me you've been watching those YouTube dance videos again," Dad grinned. But the twins had to admit it—Father Miguel was a pretty awesome dancer!

Maybe, thought Patrick to himself, *it wouldn't be totally horrible to be a priest someday...*

▲ Chapter Six ▲

Dad and Katie headed off to the back pews to begin dusting and organizing the big, heavy books that held the Bible readings and songs. This left Patrick and two other Cleaning Team ladies standing near the altar with Father Miguel.

The priest considered all the jobs on Mrs. Danks's carefully prepared checklist. "It looks like the confessionals need a good cleaning," he said. "They will be busy next week. If each of you could take one, we'll be done in no time," suggested the pastor to Patrick and the two women standing next to him.

"You take mine, Patrick," offered Father Miguel. "It's the last one on the right near where your dad and Katie are working." He tossed Patrick a fresh rag and some lemony-smelling spray. "And don't forget to dust my section," he called out as Patrick was heading down the aisle.

Patrick bent, picked up his backpack, and threw it over his shoulder. Inside it, he heard Francis begin to croak with excitement. That dark space might be the perfect spot for the frog to get in a bit of jumping practice.

The wooden door creaked as Patrick pulled on the center knob between the two curtained side sections. St. Anne's was an old church with wooden confessionals that looked a little bit like closets. You could either kneel behind a wooden screen or do your confession "face-to-face" with the priest through a curtain that slid to the side.

Patrick decided to take his time, hoping the hour would be up before he was given a second job. He sat for a minute on Father Miguel's seat. The comfy old green cushion had a velvet texture that reminded him a little bit of soft, summer grass.

Patrick saw a small light near the ceiling and flipped it on. At his feet was an old book, open to a page near the middle. Plopping back onto the cushion, Patrick decided to take a peek.

Patrick saw the front pocket of the backpack bulge a bit as Francis shifted, anxious to get out. "Just hang out a couple of minutes, buddy," Patrick whispered. "Let's move this big old book so you can get some exercise…"

"*Butler's Lives of the Saints*," Patrick read out loud quietly, taking a closer look at the book. "Let's see, Francis…March 17th. St. Patrick…" He smiled at the thought that Father Miguel had been reading about his own patron saint. "Patrick" was Father Miguel's middle name. That was another reason Patrick thought his pastor

was cool. Father Miguel's family had come from Mexico, but the priest's mother had given her son an Irish saint's name.

Feeling Francis settle back down inside the backpack, Patrick turned to the book again and began to read. He leaned back and relaxed. With that lemony smell and the humming of the vacuum nearby, Patrick's eyelids grew heavy. "Maybe a little nap," he whispered to the tree frog. Outside, Patrick heard the bells of St. Anne's begin to toll their noontime call to prayer.

*Clang, clang, clang…t*he bells chimed loudly.

An hour to go, Patrick thought, settling back for a nap.

Three more bells chimed, and Patrick noticed the floor of the old church begin to rumble. With the last three chimes, the confessional door blew open in a strong rush of cold wind. Patrick jumped and tried to call for his dad.

And suddenly, everything became a blur.

▲ Chapter Seven ▲

Patrick covered his face against the cold wind. An instant later, the chiming and rumbling and blurring stopped. All was silent, until Patrick suddenly heard…

Clank, clank…

Baaaaaa…

Clank, clank…

Baaaaaa…

Patrick listened to the strange sounds. He felt the cold, wet ground beneath him before he had even opened his eyes. He shivered in the strong breeze. A mixed smell of grass, mud, and some kind of animal filled his nose. Patrick opened his eyes and spotted his blue backpack on the ground beside him. Checking the pocket for Francis, he was relieved to find his frog friend shaking but OK. He looked around in confusion and amazement. He was in a wide green field!

Patrick tried to stand up. But his legs were shaky too. He was freezing and scared. More than scared, really. Patrick was terrified.

"Katie?" Patrick yelled into the open air. "Dad?" He was starting to panic. "Father Miguel!" his voice cracked as he held back tears.

The ground around him was full of muck, rocks, and puddles. Sniffling, he saw he was surrounded by a small herd of black-faced sheep. Their dark wool was damp. Rain fell everywhere. Patrick felt like he was wearing a wet blanket.

Next to him, he spotted the tiniest lamb of the flock. The tough little lamb eyed him and then head-butted Patrick in the back. Patrick didn't know whether to laugh or cry. The lamb was full of attitude. The largest sheep wore a big bell around its neck. *That would explain the clanking noise,* Patrick thought to himself.

"Oh, don't be worrying yourself about Adhamh," came a man's voice with a strange accent from somewhere up the hill. "He doesn't mean you any troubles, lad. He's just looking to make a new friend."

Patrick pulled his backpack from between the little lamb's teeth. He struggled into a standing position. He definitely wasn't in St. Anne's anymore.

Where exactly he was, he had no idea.

As far as Patrick could see were grassy fields filled with dark rocks and black sheep. In the distance he could see long, low fences that looked like they were made of the same rocks.

The few buildings Patrick spotted looked more like shacks than houses. Their roofs were made of brown hay. The clouds were hanging low, almost touching the ground.

Patrick had no idea where he was or how he'd gotten there. He was cold, hungry, and completely freaked out. Tears dripped from his eyes, and his stomach felt like it was tied in a million knots.

Patrick tried to imagine what Katie might do if she were here. She was always so calm and in charge. He wished Katie were with him now.

"Where the heck are we, Francis?" Patrick whispered. "And how did we get here?" For some reason, in this situation, talking to a frog didn't seem weird at all.

"Ribbit," came a low, nervous-sounding croak in return.

▲ Chapter Eight ▲

"All right, my sheep friends," the voice called from up the hill. It was calling out in the direction of the bleating sheep. "Nothing to see here, so quit your complaining."

Patrick could clearly understand the words he heard. But something about the way they sounded was very strange. Sort of old-fashioned, with a funny accent. In fact, the accent reminded him of Mrs. Danks.

Looking up, Patrick saw the dark-haired stranger begin to walk towards him. He scanned the field, realizing that there was really nowhere for him

to hide. Running away seemed impossible. Fear made his arms and legs feel even colder.

The stranger had a long stick in his hand. The stick had a kind of hook at the top. A few stray sheep were following behind him as he came. Patrick thought he should be scared, but something about the guy made him feel at ease.

"Welcome!" he said as he got close to Patrick. "I see you've met Adhamh! Don't worry, he won't eat you. He's just saying hello. We don't get many visitors in this place. But you are welcome here."

"And where, *exactly,* is here?" Patrick asked, backing away from the shepherd.

"Why, Ireland, of course!" answered the young man. Now he sounded confused, too. He was looking at Patrick, noticing the hoodie and the backpack.

"No way!" Patrick took several steps away from the stranger.

"I can tell you are not from around here," the shepherd said. "Your clothes, and the way you speak…. I don't know how you came to be here. But, don't be afraid, lad. I mean you no harm. It seems God led us to this muddy field together! I was just getting ready for my prayers and a bit of food. Won't you join me? We will eat."

Oh great, thought Patrick to himself. *I may not be at church, but I still have to pray. Actually, I really need to pray! Where am I?* He felt the panic inside him start to rise up again.

"What do you call yourself, lad?" the shepherd asked.

"Patrick," the boy answered, clutching the frog to his chest. "And this is Francis. And we need to get home—now! My parents are going to be so freaked out when they find out what happened…"

"Listen, Patrick," the shepherd spoke soothingly.

"I know what it's like to be lost and afraid. Let us feed you and get you dry, and warm. And then we will figure out how to get you home."

Since he was starving and it was quickly getting dark, Patrick agreed. But to be safe, as the shepherd turned his back, Patrick picked up a large black stone and put it into his backpack. "Just in case," he whispered to Francis.

▲ Chapter Nine ▲

Keeping a good distance between them, Patrick followed the shepherd to a small clearing in the grass. The young man set a few sticks and some clumps of something that looked like brick on top of a burned-out fire. Rubbing two sticks together, the shepherd sparked a small flame. Then fell to his knees in the mud.

"Heavenly Father," he called out, his arms outstretched to the sky. Patrick stood by, watching without really joining in. Somehow, he felt too lost to pray. And he'd never seen someone pray like this before—out in the middle of a field, like he was just having a regular conversation with God. No sign of the cross, just talking…it reminded Patrick of the way he talked to Dad when something was bugging him or when he had an important question.

"I thank you for this day," the shepherd prayed. "I thank you for the rain, which greens this grass. I thank you for my sheep, who keep me company. I thank you for the beauty of all of your creation and for the simple food you have sent to nourish us. I pray for the strength to do your will, today and always. Father, we pray for Patrick, that he may safely make his way home to his loved ones."

"Amen," said Patrick, making the Sign of the Cross. "That last part can't happen soon enough." He moved forward a little. The fire felt warm and inviting.

"Do you have a cell phone I can use?" he asked.

"What is a cell phone?" the young man replied curiously.

No cell phones in Ireland? Not good, Patrick thought, feeling the panic start again.

"Look," he said, trying to sound calm, "I need to call my family. I've got to get home. *Now.* It's already dark and I'm sure my mom is super mad at me by now…"

The shepherd answered as he poked the fire with a stick. "I'm afraid you'll have to stay here tonight. There are no homes for many miles. Tomorrow, we will make a plan. We will make our way to a place where you can send your family a message."

Patrick looked out into the darkness. He realized he would have to trust the shepherd's plan. He had no idea how he had gotten here, but he felt sure that it must have been God. And if God brought him here, then all he could do was hope that God would bring him home.

"Is this where you live?" Patrick asked, finally allowing himself to sit down. "I don't see your house."

"I sleep under God's stars," the shepherd responded, "with his majesty spread over me like a warm blanket."

"But why?" Patrick pressed. He wasn't in the mood for a camping trip in the rain.

"It's complicated..." the young man responded as he placed some cut-up potatoes and carrots into a small pot of water over the fire. "I used to live very far from here. I had a fancy home, rich clothing, and was never hungry. But even though I miss my parents, my life is much happier now."

"How?" Patrick challenged. "It's terrible here. It's freezing, muddy, and there are these noisy, smelly sheep all over the place!"

"Baaaaa!" wailed Adhamh, clearly not happy with Patrick's opinion.

"I was brought here six years ago when I was kidnapped—stolen away from my family by a band of raiders," the shepherd told him.

"Raiders? You mean like pirates or something?" Patrick imagined the movies he and Katie had watched.

"It happened very suddenly. There was yelling and fighting and a terrible trip by sea."

"What did you do?"

"At first, I was very frightened, and very angry. I lost all hope that I would ever see my family again. My parents and grandparents were holy, but even though they tried to teach me about God, I wasn't interested in anything except having a good time with my friends."

"What's wrong with that?" Patrick asked, poking the fire with a stick he had found. He had moved in just a little closer to it as the shepherd was telling his story.

"I didn't know then what I know now. I have learned to love God in this place. Even though I must work for the Druid chief priest Milchu, my life is truly blessed."

"Milchu's a priest?" asked Patrick, wondering if maybe Milchu knew Father Miguel and could help him to get back to St. Anne's.

"Not the kind of priest you might be thinking of," answered the shepherd. "He is a Druid. The people of this land do not know the one true God. I used to be just like them. My parents told me about God, but I never really believed. Even so, God protected me. He took care of me as a father does his son. Now I love him with all my heart."

"Even here?" Patrick asked, looking around him at the darkening field.

"In this place, I have come to know and love God. I stop my work a hundred times a day to pray and talk to God. This land is lovely to me, because it was here that I came to know God's love for me—indeed for all of us."

Patrick thought about what the shepherd had said. He also thought about what Katie would do in this situation. She would pray. But Patrick doubted that praying would do him any good. He had prayed with his family lots of times, but God always felt so distant.

Patrick remembered how the shepherd had prayed, as if God were right there with them. *Could God really hear me in this place?* Patrick wondered.

After he finished his meal, Patrick curled up on the ground next to the fire with Adhamh on one side and Francis on the other tucked safely into the backpack.

Looking up at the stars, he tried to figure out how he could have possibly gotten here. Was he kidnapped like the shepherd? Maybe someone had knocked him out in the confessional and somehow brought him here! Would he have to spend the rest of his life being a shepherd too?

Would he ever feel warm again, or have enough to eat, or see his family?

Finally, after a long time, Patrick drifted off into a restless sleep with a prayer of his own on his lips.

"God, I am lost…I'm like a lost sheep. Help me to find my way home…"

▲ Chapter Ten ▲

"Wake up, young one…" a voice whispered with urgency. "We must be going!"

Patrick's eyes opened in the darkness. For a moment he completely forgot where he was. Clutching his backpack to his chest to protect Francis, he had rolled himself into a ball on the hard ground. The fire was now almost completely out. Patrick's heart beat heavily in his chest, and he shivered with cold. He looked around trying to figure out where he could possibly be.

Then he remembered everything that had happened in the last several hours.

He was in the middle of a field in Ireland.

He was with a total stranger.

His parents had no idea where he was.

He had to get home!

"Come on!" the shepherd nudged him again. "We must be going, now! There's no time to lose. It will be morning soon."

"Wait a minute," Patrick protested. "I'm not going anywhere until I figure out what's going on. Who are you really, and where are we going?"

"There's no time now!" the shepherd said impatiently. "I will tell you my story later, as we're walking. When we get to safety, we will return you to your parents. I promise you. But for now, if we have any hope of escaping this place, we must run."

The shepherd turned quickly. His sheep huddled around him. They seemed to know that their caretaker was leaving them.

Weirdest group hug ever! thought Patrick to himself. It would have been funny if it hadn't been so strange. He listened as the young man called to out to his sheep.

"I must leave you now my sheep, but I thank you. I hated you at first. So often, I felt alone and hopeless. But you were always with me, and God was too. I leave you now to God's protection."

Turning to Patrick, he called with urgency, "Come, lad, we must be away!"

▲ Chapter Eleven ▲

And so the two of them took off at a run. The shepherd carried only his long stick, a shepherd's crook, and Patrick had nothing but his backpack and Francis.

They ran for an hour, until Patrick finally dropped to the ground. "I can't go any more! I am starving, wet, and freezing. *Where are we? And where* are we going? I'm not taking one more step until I get some answers."

The shepherd nodded, acknowledging his own exhaustion, too.

"I told you, I came to Ireland as a slave," the shepherd began in a worried voice. "I was taken by force from my home when I was only sixteen. I was young and selfish and foolish back then. I came to this place, Ireland, where I have served my master for six long years."

"Six years?" Patrick was confused. "How could you possibly be a slave? People don't have slaves anymore."

Patrick felt a very strange racing in his heart. He had a suspicion… But no! *It couldn't be!*

"What year is this?" Patrick asked. "You said we are in Ireland, but what year is this?"

The shepherd looked at the young boy in the strange clothing with his odd blue bag on his shoulders. He considered the small creature the boy carried with him, the one the boy kept calling "Francis." The shepherd felt confused too.

"While I have only tracked time by the rising and setting of the sun, I believe this to be the year of our Lord 395."

Patrick burst out laughing. "395? Impossible!"

Then Patrick's mind flashed back to St. Anne's.

The bells chiming…

The ground rumbling…

That cold wind…

Could it be? Time travel?

"How will we ever get home?" Patrick asked the shepherd in a frightened voice. He felt like screaming. "How will I ever find my family?"

"It's a question I ask myself every day, young one," the shepherd replied, not really answering Patrick's question at all. "But tonight, God has answered my prayers. For tonight, I had an amazing dream, a vision, really."

"A dream?" Patrick scowled. "You wake me up, drag me through a forest in the pitch dark. I have no idea where we're going! And now you tell me it's all because of a dream? I don't need visions. I need to get home!"

"That's it, lad," the shepherd said, trying to calm him. "This is why I ran away from my master. In my vision, I heard a voice talking to me."

"What did the voice say?" Patrick asked.

The shepherd began to tell Patrick about his dream. "The voice said, 'You have fasted well. Very soon you will return to your native country.' At first, I thought it was simply my imagination. I tried to go back to sleep. But then again, the voice said to me, 'Look—your ship is ready.'"

"So now we're running around in the middle of the night trying to find a ship?" Patrick said, beginning to panic. How could he tell this slave that he was not only lost, but also lost in time? The last thing he needed was to have the only person who could help him going crazy.

"Do not fear, my friend," the shepherd said calmly. "God is with us; he will guide us both home. We will find my ship. We will return you to your family. I swear to you that you will be under my protection. Let's pray for the safety of our journey."

Patrick sighed, but knelt in the muddy grass beside the shepherd, feeling his fear lessen as they began to pray. The shepherd called upon God to protect them on their journey.

After they had prayed, Patrick looked the shepherd in the eye and made the decision to trust him. This man called on God. He seemed genuinely worried about Patrick. And Patrick needed to tell *someone* what had happened. The boy told the shepherd his whole story.

Francis jumping into the font.

The bells.

The rumbling and wind.

Everything.

And the shepherd, who began to understand the boy's strange clothing and way of speaking, listened. Then he asked questions.

As the sun rose, Patrick shared about his family. He smiled, telling the shepherd about how Katie always had a plan for everything. "I'm pretty sure she would know how to get home if she were here," he said.

"Then we must think like Katie. We must plan," the shepherd said, trying to calm Patrick. "And we must trust that if you came to be here in this place and in this time, there must be a way for you and Francis to return home again."

▲ Chapter Twelve ▲

For the next several days, the pair walked, and walked, and walked. For what felt like hundreds of miles, they climbed up and down hills in the wind, rain, and fog. They had nothing to eat but the food they found along the way, which the shepherd cooked over an open fire.

Patrick's shoes, new at the start of this year's basketball season, were now covered in mud and falling to pieces. He felt hungry all of the time.

And he worried for poor Francis, who didn't seem to be growing like he should. The weather in Ireland was cold and wet. The wind blew all the time. With each day that passed, Francis seemed weaker.

Patrick began to give up hope that he and Francis would ever get home to his family. But through it all, "Shep"—as Patrick had started calling his mysterious new protector—told him stories. Every time Patrick felt like he wanted to give up, Shep would remind him of God's love and protection. He truly believed that if God had brought Patrick here, God would get him home.

And in a way that Patrick had never felt before, he began to understand that God was truly with him. Even in this terrible situation. Every day along their path, they would find kind people who helped them. Some offered the little bits of food that they could spare. Others gave them shelter.

After days on the road, one very nice family invited Shep, Patrick, and Francis to sleep on a bed of hay in their very small cottage. The Collins family had never seen a frog before. They immediately fell in love with Francis. Patrick realized that although Mr. and Mrs. Collins and their kids were very poor, they were also very generous.

Finally, Patrick, Francis, and Shep arrived at a town on the edge of the water. There, waiting in the harbor, was a large boat. Patrick watched from a hiding spot as the shepherd approached it.

"I need to sail with you!" Shep called out to the captain of the ship.

"Don't you dare try to come with us!" the captain yelled. Patrick could tell that the captain was not the type to take pity on a lost shepherd, a kid, or even a frog named Francis. Now what would they do?

Shep walked away from the ship, joining Patrick where he was hiding. "We will go back to the Collinses' cottage until I decide what step we should take next."

"What's wrong?" Patrick asked, his voice revealing his fear. "We've come so far and walked so many miles to get here!"

"Ribbit," croaked Francis.

As they walked away from the ship, someone shouted at Shep.

"Come quickly—those men are calling you!"

So they headed back to the ship. Patrick and Francis stood out of sight, watching what happened next.

"Come—we'll trust you. Prove you're our friend any way you wish," said one of the ship's mates to Shep.

The sailors were loud, terrible men. They took turns teasing Shep, yelling and calling him horrible names. They told the shepherd that he could board their ship, but their eyes were cruel and threatening.

But Shep refused to be afraid of these men. He would rather not board the ship than join with them in going against God's teachings.

Something about Shep's courage must have impressed the rowdy sailors. They took mercy on him and invited him aboard. The told him the journey across the sea was about to begin. "We need someone as brave as you aboard this ship!"

"But wait," said Patrick, as he saw the shepherd preparing to board the boat. "What about me? You promised that you would help me! And now you're just going to take off with these guys? How am I supposed to get home?"

"I've made a plan for you, Patrick!" Shep consoled him. "Return to the cottage where we slept last night. The Collins family has agreed to help you find your parents. They are kind people. You can trust them to feed and shelter you until you find your way home."

"Hold on!" Patrick yelled. "You can't just leave me here! We've come all this way and I'm still no closer to getting home to my family. You haven't told me *anything* except how much you love God. Come on, Shep, I don't even know your real name!"

"Patrick, if God brought you to this place and time, then God has a plan to see you home. As much as I would like to take you with me, I don't truly trust these sailors. They could throw both of us overboard."

"So you want me to just wait here?" Patrick couldn't believe this was happening.

"Trust in the Lord, young one," Shep called as the boat's anchor was pulled up and her moorings were untied. "God has a plan for your life, just as he has one for mine. I am leaving you here, but you will be safe. You will unlock the secret of what brought you here in God's time. Be patient, and you will see God's plan unfold."

And with the sound of the ship's bell ringing overhead, the young shepherd turned back to Patrick with a few last words…

"You asked for my name. My parents called me *Maewyn Succat*. But I've decided that once I find my way to freedom, God is calling me to be a priest. I will return here to Ireland to serve the Irish. I will share my love for God with these people who have never known the true God.

Please pray for me, that I can help people to find the love of Jesus Christ in their hearts. I will pray for you and Francis, lad. You *will* find your way home to your people."

Shep continued, in the middle of the clanging of the ship's bell and the sound of sea birds in the wind.

"As a priest, I will have a new name," he yelled to the boy. "So you can call me 'Patricius,' or simply 'Patrick'..."

▲ Chapter Thirteen ▲

Patrick stood on the shore watching Patricius sail away.

"Patricius?" he asked Francis. "Ireland? 395?"

An Irish shepherd? Named Patrick? Patrick's mind raced back to the confessional, to Father Miguel's book.

Had he just walked across Ireland with St. Patrick?

Patrick decided on a plan, just like Katie would do. He would find some food for Francis. He would walk to Collinses' cottage. He would find a way to get home…

As he stood in the harbor preparing to start the long walk to the cottage, a nearby sailor from another ship approached him.

"Aye, lad, let us have a peek in that blue satchel of yours," the man said. He smelled terrible. He grabbed for Patrick's backpack.

Inside the pack, Francis croaked weakly. The man's grimy hands were coming dangerously close to the little frog.

In an instant, Patrick reached in his pocket, as he yelled at the sailor, "Get away from me!" With his heart racing, he pulled out the black rock he had picked up on his first night in Ireland. He'd been carrying it for miles. Taking aim, Patrick threw the rock straight in the face of the nasty sailor.

AYY!

ouch!

The rock hit with a terrible thud. The sailor fell over hard, holding his eye.

Patrick scooped up the backpack and ran as fast as he'd ever run. Nearby, more sailors noticed him and began to chase him away from the harbor.

Patrick dodged between the carts and animals and through the puddles that filled the streets. With his pack on his back, he ran and ran and ran until finally he was out of the town and back on the path to the cottage.

Before long, hunger and tiredness finally overtook him. Remembering what Patricius had taught him along their journey, Patrick stuffed himself with as many safe wild berries as he could find. Then he found a small, dry clearing alongside a rock wall.

"We'll rest here for a little while, Francis," Patrick said, trying to sound confident. "And then we will find Mr. and Mrs. Collins."

Somehow, reassuring Francis made Patrick feel less afraid. Patrick knew that Francis needed to be protected. Focusing on his little frog helped him feel as though he had a plan.

So, after finding a few crickets and worms for Francis to eat, Patrick found a small area next to a spring where his pet could jump around in safety. He knew that Francis needed exercise. But he also knew the weather in this place was too cold for a frog. One more reason both of them had to figure out how to get back to St. Anne's as soon as possible!

As Patrick placed Francis back in the pocket of his backpack, the frog let out a low, weak-sounding croak.

"It's OK, little guy," Patrick whispered, trying his best to sound like Dad, who was the bravest man he knew. "We'll sleep at the Collinses' cottage tonight. Then, we'll get home tomorrow morning, as soon as the sun comes up."

This seemed to satisfy Francis, who snuggled into the bed of moss that Patrick had fixed for him in the backpack. He knew his pet couldn't last much longer under these circumstances.

Patrick wasn't really sure what he'd do when he woke up the next morning. He thought of Patricius. He still didn't feel comfortable calling Shep "Patrick." He thought about his patron saint. He'd known St. Patrick was from Ireland, but he never imagined he'd actually *meet* him!

Patrick's stomach growled. He felt scared and lonely. But then he remembered what Patricius had told him. He'd been just like Patrick—alone and afraid and really far away from his family. And somehow, even in all of that trouble, the shepherd had found God. His faith had helped to save him!

"Maybe I should try praying on my own, Francis," Patrick reasoned. "It definitely couldn't hurt…"

▲ Chapter Fourteen ▲

Patrick got on his knees, as he'd seen Patricius do so many times during their journey to the ship.

"In the name of the Father, and of the Son, and of the Holy Spirit, Amen," Patrick recited from memory. He went on to say an Our Father and ten Hail Marys, almost as fast as Mrs. Danks could say them.

Then Patrick waited for a minute, trying to see if anything felt different.

It didn't.

"What am I doing wrong, Francis?" Patrick sighed. "I'm praying to go home! Why isn't God hearing me? Maybe God's not even really out there!"

Then Patrick remembered something he had heard Patricius say.

One night along their journey to the ship, Shep had told him about how he had been able to survive so many lonely nights as a slave.

"God guarded me before I knew him," Patricius had said that night by the fire. "God protected me and consoled me as a father does his son."

When Shep had spoken these words to Patrick, the boy didn't really have a clue what he was trying to say to him. Now, in his fear and loneliness, Patrick suddenly understood. He and Francis were not here alone—God was with them. "As much as Mom and Dad love me," Patrick realized, "God loves me even more. He is guarding me. He is with me."

So Patrick tried again, this time deciding to use his own words instead of prayers he had memorized at school.

"God? It's me, Patrick," the boy whispered, sounding hopeful for the first time in days. "And Francis is here too, God…"

"Patricius told me that when he was a slave, he learned to talk to you in prayer. He said he talked to you a hundred times a day. He's told me so much about you—about how you know and love us just the way we are.

"Well, here's the deal, God," Patrick continued, growing a little more confident. He got off his knees and began to walk in circles near the stone wall. "I know I've messed up a lot of times. I've been mean. I've done dumb stuff. I know I've made a lot of stupid mistakes…"

"I shouldn't have been so mean to Gregory, God," Patrick continued. "And I probably shouldn't fight with Katie so much. I know I could help out more around home, too. Mom's so busy! And, well, taking Francis to church even when I know I'm not supposed to… "

As Patrick paused, Francis let out a soft croak.

"But I need to get home, God," Patrick prayed out loud. "I'm not even really sure how I got here in the first place. Everything is so strange, so old-fashioned. And I'm cold and tired. I know that my parents are probably really worried about me…"

At that thought, his voice cracked as he felt tears welling up.

Patrick closed his eyes.

"I know that you love me, and I truly love you, too, God…" Patrick prayed. But a low sound interrupted him. He couldn't quite figure out what it was. But the sound was coming closer. He kept his eyes shut tight and focused on his prayer.

"And I'm asking you, with all my heart," Patrick continued praying, noticing the ground begin to rumble. "Please God, help me get home to my family. If you'll help me, I promise to…"

Patrick heard the sound again. "A bell chiming?" he asked Francis. "Out here in the middle of nowhere. *What could it be?*"

Then a strong rush of cold wind blew, pushing Patrick and Francis with its force.

And suddenly everything became a blur.

▲ Chapter Fifteen ▲

An instant later, the chiming and rumbling and blurring became still. Patrick's heart raced, then dropped into his stomach as he figured out that he still wasn't back at St. Anne's.

Everything was silent, until Patrick heard a noise…

Dongety-dong, dongety-dong, dongety-dong…

The ringing bell was clearly getting closer. Patrick, peering over the top of the rock wall, saw a tall, brown-robed old man ringing what looked like a big cowbell. In his other hand, the man held a long staff, a lot like Patricius's shepherd's crook. Behind him were two other, younger men. They also wore those long brown robes.

Patrick would have laughed if he hadn't been so scared of that long stick they had. He crouched, hiding and listening to their conversation.

"But are you certain that we must go there first? To the land of your former master, the Druid king Milchu?" the followers asked the old man. The fear in their voices was obvious. "Surely he will throw you in prison or kill you for escaping."

Dongety-dong, dongety-dong, dongety-dong...

The bell sound was now very close to Patrick's hiding spot. Patrick reached into the backpack quietly, checking on Francis. He looked around, making an escape plan.

That's when he noticed that this place looked weird. Something had changed. The nearby trees were taller. The rock wall looked newer, as if someone had come along and put more rocks on top of the ones that had already been there. Even the grass seemed greener, and there were more wildflowers. It was like the time of year had changed.

Patrick's hands shook. He tried to figure out the best possible way to get out of there without being seen.

"Do not be afraid, my brothers," Patrick heard the tall man say. He was ringing that bell he held in his left hand. "With God, all things are possible…. I must return to the land of my former master and pay to him the ransom for my life. And then, we will journey all over Ireland spreading the Good News!"

"We will follow you," the men with him answered. "Through you we have come to know the one true God. We trust you, Bishop."

Dongety-dong, dongety-dong, dongety-dong…

Bishop? Patrick thought. He had only met a bishop once, a few years ago at St. Anne's. He remembered the bishop's tall pointy hat and that golden stick he'd held in his hand at Mass…

"Why, hello. Who is this? A young lad…" came the old man's voice from over the top of his hiding place. Suddenly Patrick saw the bishop, standing in front of him. A look of surprise crossed the old man's face.

"Praise be to God. I have been looking for you, Patrick!"

Patrick stood up from behind the rock. The man he saw in front of him looked a little bit like Patricius, only much older.

"Hello, sir," Patrick smiled. He couldn't help himself. It was strange, but he had an idea.

The bells chiming…

…the rumbling…

…the wind?

"Could it be?" Patrick said. "Have we traveled in time again?"

Somehow, even though it didn't make any sense, and he had only been alone for a short time, Patrick knew.

"Are you Patricius?"

▲ Chapter Sixteen ▲

A smile crossed the bishop's face. It was clear that years and years had passed for Bishop Patricius. And yet Patrick and Francis looked exactly the same. They greeted each other as old friends. Patrick was so relieved not to be alone anymore!

Patrick agreed to travel with the bishop. He was hoping that somehow, staying with Bishop Patrick would help him unlock whatever secret was needed to make another jump in time.

"Um, do you mind telling me how you suddenly got so…old?" Patrick asked the bishop as they walked together. The bishop's priest friends and some other young men they had met along the way followed behind them.

"I have so much to tell you, Patrick," the bishop answered. "So much has happened since we were last together."

"But you just left on the boat," Patrick wondered out loud. "And I was worried about you. That crew looked pretty creepy."

"It was quite a journey," the bishop remembered. They walked along the rocky path. Bishop Patrick shared what had happened after they had separated from each other. Patrick quit trying to figure out the time travel part. Instead, he simply chose to listen to the bishop's incredible adventure.

"After three days we made it to land," Bishop Patrick explained. "Then for twenty-eight days we traveled through the wilderness. All of our food ran out. Everyone was starving. The captain looked at me one day and said, 'What about this, Christian? You tell us that your God is great and all-powerful—why can't you pray for us, since we're all starving? Will your God help us?'

"I trusted in God," Bishop Patrick continued. "So I said to them: 'Have faith in God, because nothing is impossible for him!'

"With the help of God, a miracle happened!" Bishop Patrick continued. "A herd of pigs appeared right before our eyes! The sailors hunted many of them. We camped there for two nights. We had more than enough to eat, even the dogs! After this, the sailors all gave thanks to God. I was honored in their eyes. From this day on, they had plenty of food."

Patrick considered how close the bishop had come to danger. And yet it seemed like he had not even been afraid!

"And how on earth did you go from almost becoming lunch for that crew to becoming a bishop?" Patrick asked in disbelief. It seemed like Shep, Patricius, Bishop Patrick—or whatever this guy was calling himself—always seemed to find the right answers to his problems. Since God always seemed to keep Bishop Patrick safe, Patrick thought it was a good idea to stay close and follow his lead.

"God is truly so good, my friend," the bishop continued. "I was able to return safely to my family. They had missed me so much. They begged me to never leave them again."

Patrick could relate to that! He knew that when he finally made it home, after his parents grounded him for the rest of his life, they would both give him the biggest hugs in the world. He missed baby Hoa Hong so much, even her crying!

And Katie? Patrick couldn't wait to share this adventure with his twin. He knew that she must be so worried about him. Patrick wanted to get home and see her and tell her all about Ireland.

"So how did you end up back here?" Patrick asked.

"One night, when I had returned to my family," Bishop Patrick answered, "I had a vision about a man named Victorius. He had come to me from Ireland with hundreds of letters—so many I could not even count them. He gave me one of the letters. As I read it, I heard the voice of the Irish people. They called out as if with one voice: 'We beg you, holy boy, to come and walk again among us.' This touched my heart deeply. I could not read any more. And then I woke up. Thanks be to God, after many years the Lord granted them what they were asking for. And here I am!"

"So you became a priest, and then a bishop?" Patrick asked. Father Miguel had once taught the boys in his class about becoming a priest. Patrick had sort of zoned out that day, since he always thought it would be better to be a professional soccer player than a priest.

"My heart is truly with the people of this land," the bishop explained to Patrick. "I will live out the rest of my days here. I have come to Ireland to spread the Good News of the Gospel!"

▲ Chapter Seventeen ▲

The group arrived in a clearing nearby the druid priest Milchu's property. In the distance, Patrick saw a flock of sheep grazing. As they approached, the largest ram turned toward them. Suddenly, the ram began to run, the bell around his neck clanging with every step.

"Ahhh, my Adhamh," Bishop Patrick held out his hands to the ram. "You have become the bell sheep!"

"What is a bell sheep?" Patrick asked, Adhamh's clanging ringing in his ears. He couldn't believe the sassy little lamb had suddenly become the leader of the flock.

"A good shepherd knows each one of his flock," explained Bishop Patrick. "He watches his sheep to see the one who follows him most closely. Around the neck of that sheep, he hangs a bell. Where the bell sheep goes, the others will follow. Adhamh, like his father before him, leads his brothers and sisters along the path to food, shelter, and safety. He is the bell sheep."

That makes sense, Patrick thought to himself. "Speaking of food and shelter," he said to Bishop Patrick, his stomach growling, "It's getting dark out. Isn't it time for us to stop for the night? I know you don't want to go see Milchu in the middle of the night!"

"You are right, my son," Bishop Patrick laughed. "We will rest for the night and begin our mission fresh in the morning."

With that, a fire was built, and a simple meal was shared. The small band of travelers gathered around the flames. They listened as their bishop led them in prayer. Over their heads, the stars shone brightly in the clear Irish sky. For a moment, Patrick forgot his fear and the ache he felt to be reunited with his family. In his heart, he felt a peace that was new to him.

After dinner, in the light of the fire, Bishop Patrick knelt. He picked a small shamrock from the ground. He began to teach his followers about the *Trinity*. That was a word that Patrick had heard before but never really understood.

Three persons in one God? Patrick thought to himself. *What is that supposed to mean?*

As Bishop Patrick held the small green shamrock toward the night sky, he showed them that, even though it had three separate parts, it was really only one thing.

"There is only one true God. Everything we see—and even the things we cannot see—were created by God," Bishop Patrick taught. "God sent his son, Jesus Christ, because he loved us so much. And he sends his Holy Spirit to help us to know God, since we are his children."

I am God's child, thought Patrick, his eyelids becoming heavy as he heard Adhamh's bell clanging softly in the distance.

Clank, clank...

Baaaaaa...

Patrick stared into the fire, considering all that he had learned from the Bishop. As Bishop Patrick finished his teaching, he used his silver bishop's bell to call the group to pray together.

The bell's bright chiming sound mixed with the clanging of Adhamh's bell. Patrick listened as he stared into the stars. He felt so close to God in that moment.

"Patrick, child of God..." he whispered to himself, snuggling near the fire on the grass, his backpack clutched close. Inside it, Francis croaked, sounding warm and peaceful.

With sound of Bishop Patrick and Adhamh's bells chiming in the distance, Patrick suddenly felt the ground near the fire begin to rumble.

A strong rush of cold wind blew across the pasture.

And suddenly, everything became a blur.

▲ Chapter Eighteen ▲

With a start, Patrick found himself in the darkness. He was clutching the backpack that held Francis.

Overhead, the bells of St. Anne's chimed three times. The loud rumbling shook the floor of the small space where Patrick was sitting.

For a moment, Patrick looked around in the dim lighting. He had no idea how he'd arrived there.

Within a few seconds, Patrick realized that for the first time in days he felt warm and dry. He listened for the sound of the sheep and the crackling of the fire. But instead he heard the sound of the humming vacuum outside the door.

He recognized the feel of the comfy green cushion beneath him and that familiar lemony smell in the air of the small space.

"I don't think we're in Ireland anymore, Francis," Patrick whispered. Then excitement overtook him, and he threw open the door to Father Miguel's confessional.

"I'm back!" he yelled, the sound of his excitement ringing off the old concrete walls of St. Anne's.

"Dad! Katie!" Patrick called out, running down the aisle to where his father and Katie were busily dusting the last few pews. "I'm home! It's so great to see you! Were you worried? You must have been totally freaking out! But don't worry now, Francis and I made it back safe and sound! Where's Mom and Hoa Hong? I can't wait to see them!"

In his excited chattering, Patrick didn't notice the puzzled look on his dad's face.

"Katie, you should have seen it!" Patrick shouted, gripping his twin sister in a giant bear hug. "It was amazing. So green! And you would have loved the sheep, especially little Adhamh! What a feisty guy…"

Katie looked at Patrick in shock. "What are you talking about? Have you finally lost your mind?"

"Ireland! I know you guys must have been so worried! Now that I'm home, I sort of wish I'd been there a while longer, but…"

Katie interrupted him, shaking his shoulders. "*Ireland?* Nice. Well, I was in Paris, so you should be jealous…" she said with a giggle.

"I'm serious, Katie," Patrick stopped her. "I'm not messing around."

"What are you talking about, Patrick?" Katie asked, pulling Patrick away from Dad and toward one of the long pews.

Patrick glanced over his shoulder, looking at Dad. When he was far enough away, Patrick began to tell her his story. The words came out quickly and didn't seem to make much sense.

"So you're telling me that you traveled in time, Patrick?" Katie whispered. "But how? We've only been here a few minutes. You just went into Father Miguel's confessional."

"I don't know," Patrick whispered back. "I'm really not sure. But I think it might have something to do with bells…"

Finding a place to sit down, he looked up and saw Father Miguel watching him. A hint of a smile seemed to cross the priest's face.

"Did you get my confessional cleaned up already, Patrick?" Father Miguel asked in a quiet voice that made Patrick realize how loudly he'd been speaking.

"Um….working on it, Father," Patrick answered quietly. He was trying to figure out how best to explain what he'd just experienced. He couldn't comprehend how everyone in St. Anne's was just going on with their cleaning. And where were Mom, and Hoa Hong? Surely they would have wanted to see Patrick after he'd been lost for such a long time!

"Twenty more pews, and then we'll figure out what we're doing for lunch," Dad announced. "Any requests, Patrick?"

Patrick paused, trying to figure out how to explain to his father that it had been weeks since he'd had a good meal. The memory of his hunger reminded him about his dirty clothes and shoes. But when he looked down at them, he saw that they were fresh and clean. Something wasn't adding up.

"It's all impossible," Patrick whispered to Katie. "But it really happened. I'll tell you more about it when we get home."

After the cleaning hour had passed, Patrick's head was still spinning. In the backpack, Francis seemed active and happy, like he couldn't wait to get home and stretch his legs.

Patrick looked over at Father Miguel, who was now chatting with the two Cleaning Team ladies. The boy walked up to them. He thought that talking to Father Miguel would help solve the confusion he felt.

"Thank you so much for your help, Mara and Norma," Father Miguel said, finishing up their conversation. "We'll see you on Tuesday for the parish penance service."

"Well, young Patrick," said Father Miguel, turning to the boy. "How was your first Cleaning Team mission?"

Something about the way his pastor said those words caught Patrick by surprise. Nearby, Katie looked over at the two of them standing there. The smile on her face told Patrick that she believed him, even if the whole thing seemed impossible.

"Mission?" Patrick answered back curiously.

"Seriously, Patrick, your secret is safe with me!" the priest responded with a smile. "You wouldn't be the first person to lose track of time in St. Anne's!"

▲ Chapter Nineteen ▲

Ding-dong! Ding-dong!

Mom ran to answer the doorbell, yelling, "Let's get moving, kids!" as she stopped to put on a shoe. On the other side of the door was Mrs. Danks, who had come to babysit Hoa Hong while the Brady family went to the penance service at St. Anne's.

Alone in his room, Patrick sat like a statue on his bed.

"Let's go, Patrick!" Katie yelled, entering the room without knocking.

When she saw the look on her brother's face, she stopped in her tracks.

"What's wrong, buddy?" Katie asked tenderly, sitting on the bed next to Patrick.

"What do you care?" Patrick said softly, without looking his sister in the eye.

"Come on, look at me when you say that," Katie countered, as though she could read the pain in her brother's heart. "You haven't been yourself this week, Patrick. Really, you can tell me what's wrong."

But could he, really?

He decided to take a chance.

"Have you ever really wondered about it all, Katie?" he asked, his voice shaking a little.

"About what, Patrick?" Katie asked.

"About God, and stuff…" Patrick answered hesitantly.

"Of course!" Katie giggled. "All the time. And I bet if you asked Mom and Dad, they would say the same thing. And Father Miguel, too."

"I've just been feeling bad lately," Patrick said, his voice almost a whisper. "For a long time, I wasn't really sure about the whole God thing... I mean, I love St. Anne's and Father Miguel, and everything. I like it when our family prays together. But I have these questions...

"Then, suddenly I met this guy in Ireland," Patrick continued, his throat tightening as he fought back tears. "And he seemed to have so many answers. He really, truly loved God with all his heart. And he wanted to tell everyone he met about God..."

"Are you talking about St. Patrick?" Katie asked. Even though she still doubted her twin's incredible story, Katie knew that Patrick believed that he had really, truly traveled in time.

"I don't know, I really don't, Katie," Patrick struggled, trying to explain. "I mean, it seemed like I met him. And when I was with him, I thought I had found some of the answers I was looking for. But then, it all seemed like a dream, like something that never really happened. And now I'm wondering again…and I…"

"Kids, we've got to go, *now*!" Dad called from the hallway. The twins could hear Mom honking the horn in the front yard.

"God loves us, Patrick," Katie said, looking her brother straight in the eyes. "It may not make sense to us, but that's where faith comes in…"

Honk, honk!

"We're coming," the twins yelled at the same time. With a smile, they took off running for the front door.

A few minutes later, the red van pulled into the parking lot just as the bells of St. Anne's were chiming the hour. "See?" said Dad. "We're just on time!"

The four Bradys walked into the church together as Mr. Sarkisian's choir started the opening song. Looking around, Patrick realized he was feeling calmer.

"This place really does feel a bit like home," he whispered to his twin with a smile.

Before long, it was time for the confessions to begin. Patrick stood in line outside the wooden confessional. He felt much less nervous than he'd ever been in the past before confession.

Patrick remembered his time with Francis in Ireland last Saturday. It felt like a million years ago. Patrick decided that, even if the whole thing had been a dream, it had taught him some important lessons.

In so many ways, Patrick's own story was a lot like St. Patrick's when he was a young boy. Disbelief, mistakes, sins… Patrick's time in Ireland—or wherever he had been last Saturday—had taught him that God's love for everyone really *is* strong and true.

Just like St. Patrick, Patrick had not truly believed. He had been cruel to others. He had been more worried about having a good time with his friends than being a good person.

But if there was hope for the man they called the "Apostle of Ireland," maybe there was hope for Patrick too!

Then it was time.

"Bless me, Father, for I have sinned," Patrick began, smiling at Father Miguel. "It's been a long time since my last confession. These are my sins…"

The confession went on from there. In confessing his sins to Father Miguel, Patrick felt a sense of Jesus with him, listening to all his

mistakes through the person of that holy priest.

"I want you to remember something, Patrick," Father Miguel said in a caring voice. "We all have times when we have questions or doubts. Even some of the greatest saints had times when their faith was tested. But God is with us always. And his love is unconditional, even if we're not perfect."

Patrick thought about the times he had hurt God by hurting other people. The fights he had with Katie, the times he didn't listen to Mom, the way he had been so mean to Gregory….

Confession gave Patrick the chance to fix those hurts. Confession brought him closer to the people he loved, and to God, too.

After Patrick's confession, Father Miguel quietly offered the prayer of absolution. "May God grant you pardon and peace. And I absolve you of your sins…"

Patrick felt a weight lifted as his sins were washed away by the sacrament. Kneeling next to Katie, he felt lighter than air. Patrick thought of all he had learned from St. Patrick—about truly believing and about standing up and sharing his faith with the people in his life.

"Glory be to the Father," Patrick prayed silently, "and to the Son and to the Holy Spirit. As it was in the beginning is now, and ever shall be, world without end. Amen."

Even the words of that old prayer, the "Glory Be," sounded fresh and new when he remembered the lesson St. Patrick had shared about the Trinity. Suddenly, they weren't just memorized words anymore. They were a way for Patrick to show love for a God who loved him always, just as he was. And truly loving God meant being more loving to the people around him.

Clang, clang, clang…

The bells of St. Anne's began to chime again…

Clang, clang, clang…

Patrick felt Francis stir in the front pocket of his jacket. He placed his hand inside to pet his friend Francis, the one who had been through so much with him in such a short time.

Even if it was all a dream, Patrick thought to himself.

Clang, clang, clang… the bells chimed as Patrick pulled his hand from the pocket, looking down.

He smiled looking at his palm, which held one very green tree frog…

…and one very green shamrock.

▲ The Real St. Patrick ▲

Many legends exist about the life of St. Patrick. What we do know about the history of this amazing saint come from some of his own writings. While he lived, St. Patrick wrote his *Confessio,* a history he wrote of his own life. He also wrote "Letter to the Soldiers of Coroticus," about the wrongs of slave trading in Ireland. We believe that Patrick, called *Maewyn Succat* as a child, was born in the British Isles between 385 and 390.

When he was approximately sixteen years old, Patrick was kidnapped by Irish raiders and taken into slavery in Ireland. For six years, Patrick tended sheep for his master, the Druid chieftain Milchu. In Ireland during his captivity, Patrick discovered his Catholic faith. He began to build a strong prayer life and a relationship with God. After receiving instructions in a dream, Patrick traveled over two hundred miles, eventually escaping Ireland by boat. Patrick was returned to his family. But he began to feel a strong urge to study for the priesthood. More than anything, Patrick wanted to return to Ireland to spread the Gospel.

Patrick studied for years to become a priest. He was later appointed a bishop and sent to minister to the Irish. When Patrick returned to Ireland, most of the Irish people were following the Druids who practiced a pagan religion. Instead of believing in the one true God, they worshipped many gods. Patrick spent the rest of his life preaching the gospel to the people of Ireland. He converted so many of the Irish to Christianity, introducing them to Jesus Christ and his Church, that he is often called the "Apostle of Ireland." Patrick died in 461 in Ireland. He is believed to be buried in the cemetery next to St. Patrick Cathedral in Downpatrick. We celebrate his life and legacy on March 17 every year, as we remember his love for God, the Irish people, and the faith he taught them.

▲ St. Patrick's Breastplate ▲

A traditional prayer, attributed to St. Patrick

Christ with me, Christ before me, Christ
behind me, Christ in me.
Christ beneath me, Christ above me, Christ
at my right hand, Christ on my left.
Christ where I lie, Christ where I sit, Christ
where I arise.
Christ in the heart of everyone
who thinks of me.
Christ in the mouth of everyone
who speaks to me.
Christ in every eye that sees me.
Christ in every ear that hears me.

▲ Discussion Questions ▲

1. In the opening pages of the book we meet Katie and Patrick, twins, and their adopted sister Hoa Hong. How many people are in your family? What do you know about the day of your baptism?

2. Patrick and Katie and their parents volunteer to be a part of the Cleaning Team at St. Anne's Church. Why is it important for us to help at our parish? What types of ministries would you like to participate in at your church?

3. Patrick is very unkind to his friend Gregory. Does this ever happen at your school? Why is this wrong?

4. Father Miguel is the pastor of St. Anne's Church. Who is your pastor? What are some special things about him?

5. When Patrick first meets the shepherd, he hears him praying out loud. What are some of your favorite prayers? Where are the places you go to pray to God?

6. The shepherd makes a big decision after having a dream or vision and then praying to God. How do you make big decisions in your life?

7. Patrick prays out loud to God in a moment of fear. Have you turned to God in prayer when you felt afraid or worried?

8. Bishop Patrick teaches Patrick and his other followers about the Holy Trinity. How would you describe the Trinity to a friend?

9. Fr. Miguel comes to Katie and Patrick's classroom to teach the students. Do you

know any of the priests at your parish? Have you ever spoken with them about your questions or concerns?

10. Patrick feels great grace after receiving the sacrament of reconciliation. When was your last confession, and how did it make you feel? If it has been a long time, do you think it would be good to go to confession soon? If you have not yet made your first confession, how do you feel about receiving this special sacrament?

The Chime Travelers Series

by Lisa M. Hendey

When the bells chime, get ready for adventure and fun as you join Katie and Patrick on their travels back in time to far-distant lands. The mysterious strangers they meet along the way turn out to be saints of old who become close friends who help our young travelers understand their faith a little better. Are you ready for the trip of a lifetime? Be ready when you hear the bells chime.

Available Now!

The Sign of the Carved Cross

Katie makes a new friend as she finds herself in a Native American village in the year 1675. As she settles into village life, she discovers how strong her new friend's faith is in the face of danger from her own family. As their friendship grows, Katie also learns a few things about being a better friend to others.

ISBN 978-1-61636-848-7 | $5.99

Future Adventures Are on the Way!

Join Patrick as he finds himself in Assisi and meets a young man who left a life of wealth and power to live a life of poverty and simplicity. Find out what it means to rebuild the Church as you get to know St. Francis in book three of the Chime Travelers series.

Katie finds herself on a daring escape through the streets of Assisi with a young woman who is running away from home to give her whole life in service to the poor out of her love for Jesus. Meet St. Clare in the fourth book of the Chime Travelers series.

Follow the fun at facebook.com/chimetravelerkids